The Grey Lady and
the Strawberry Snatcher

by MOLLY BANG

FOUR WINDS PRESS   NEW YORK

Published by Four Winds Press
A division of Scholastic Magazines, Inc., New York, N.Y.

Printed in the United States of America
Library of Congress Catalog Card Number: 79-21243
1 2 3 4 5 84 83 82 81 80
ISBN 0-590-07547-0

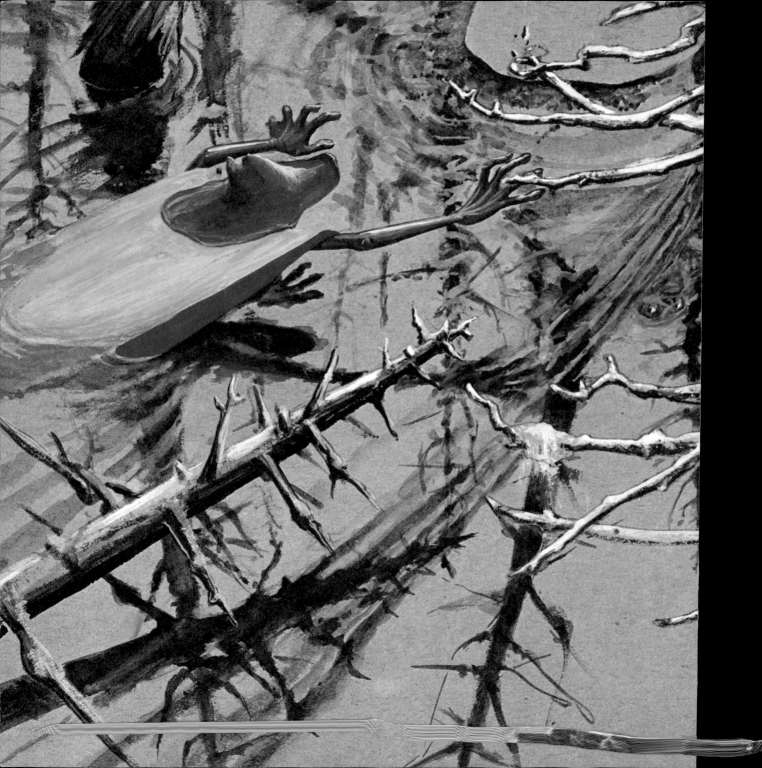

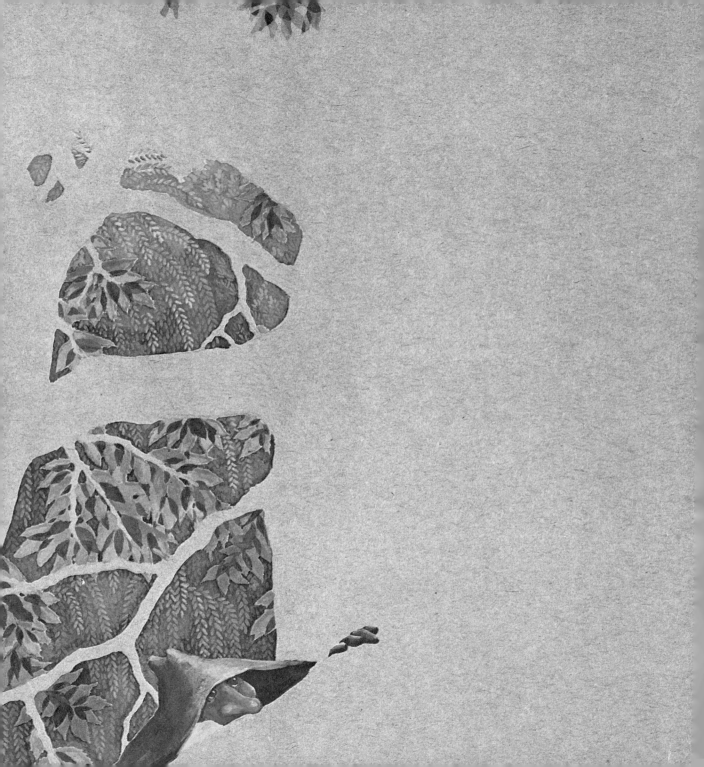

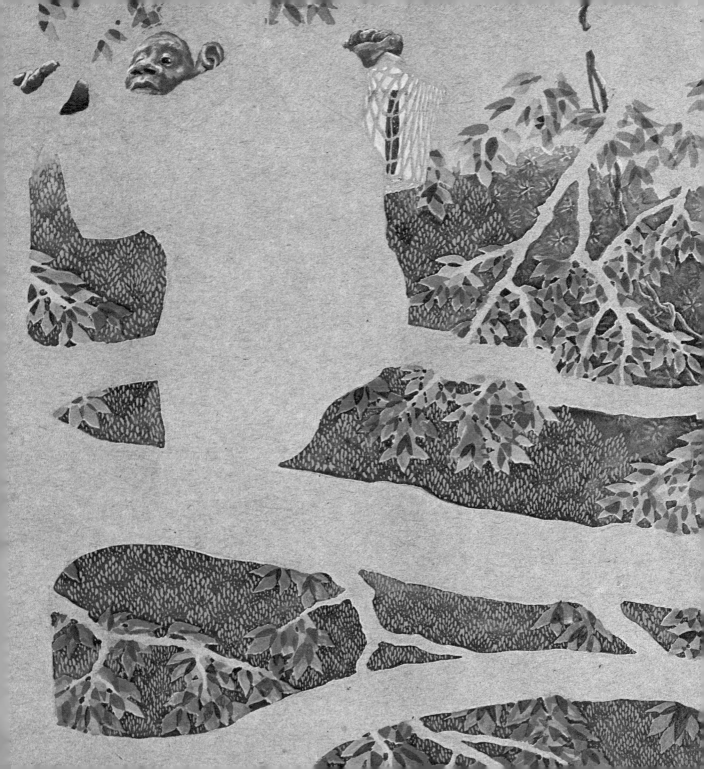

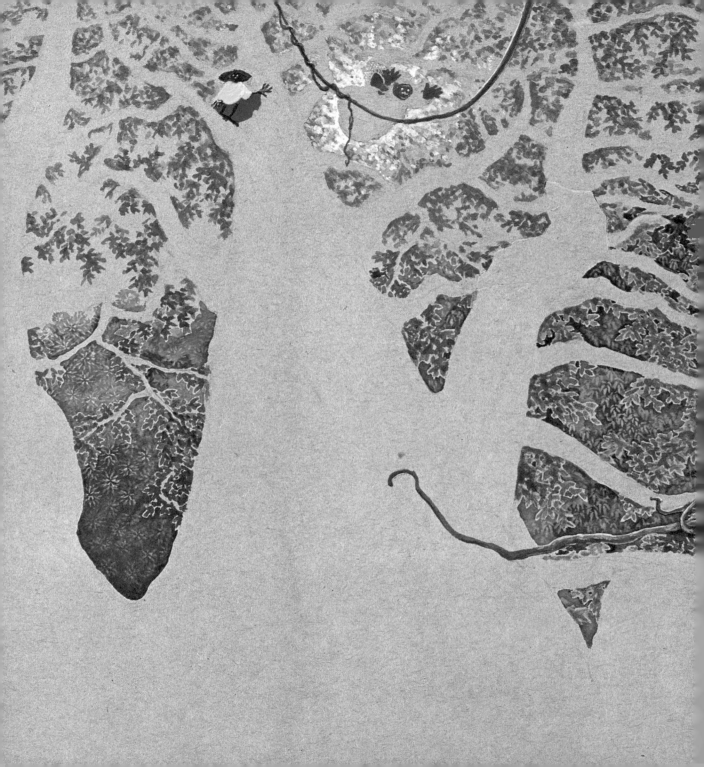